To: Tina

WHO KNEW IT
WAS BROKEN

Thanks for your
Kindness and Support.

Table of Contents

1. Family Matters

2. Crime Paid

3. Getting Out

4. Drink Up

5. A Close Call

6. The Root of All Evil

7. Atonement

Family Matters

I lay the **sins of the parents** upon their children; the entire family is affected—even children in the third and fourth generations of those who reject me.

Exodus 20:5

Jalen opened his eyes and looked around the room. He was disoriented and everything looked distorted. He blinked, trying to get a better look at who was in the room with him. If he could only turn his head, he could see better, he thought, but his head was heavy. He couldn't lift it.

"What's that noise?" Jalen heard himself say, but his lips never moved.

"Check the monitor!" Someone shouted.

The noises grew louder. There was mass confusion going on in the room and he still couldn't see clearly.

"What's going on?" The words echoed in his mind but his lips still did not move.

No one answered but the shouting continued about the monitor. He finally decided that he must be dreaming. Jalen thought about his grandmother. She used to talk about witches riding people's back in their sleep, keeping them from waking up. Maybe he needed to close his eyes and go back to sleep. His grandmother's superstitions sounded crazy but he figured a short prayer wouldn't hurt. Jalen closed his eyes and waited for sleep.

"Jalen, wake up and answer the telephone."

It was the sound of his sister's voice that woke him up. Jalen had been in a deep sleep with the covers pulled over his head. He had planned to sleep late but Raquel killed that plan, as she stood over him yelling, pressing him to answer the phone.

"Who is it?"

"Cantalope."

"Tell him I'll call him back."

"No. Get up and tell him yourself."

"Damn. I don't know why she has to be so damn difficult." Jalen mumbled to himself.

He rolled out of bed and headed for the kitchen where Raquel had left the phone off the hook. Jalen shoved her hard and she lost her balance.

"Thanks, Roc."

"Ma."

"J, keep your hands to yourself."

"All I asked her to do was tell Cantalope to call me back."

"You needed to get your butt up. Boy its one-thirty in the afternoon," his mother fired back.

Jalen picked up the phone and turned his back to them, signaling the end of that conversation.

"Hello."

"Damn man, what took you so long to get to the phone? I know you not still in the bed?"

"Man, whatever. What's up?"

"You tryin' to shoot some ball today?"

"I guess. What time?"

"Three, I guess. Is that enough time for you to get yourself together?"

"Whatever, nigga. I'll see you at three."

Jalen hung up the phone and looked at his sister who was fully dressed and on her way out. Then he looked at the clock on the stove that read 2:05. He shrugged his shoulders realizing that he had been able to sleep late.

"So, Roc, where you going?" Jalen asked.

"Daddy called he's coming by."

"What that nigga want?"

"Jalen!" said Jalen's mother. "What is wrong with you? He is still your father."

"I just don't understand why y'all get all hype because he decides he's gonna pop up."

Raquel looked at her mother and then back at her brother.

"J, when are you going to get over it?"

"Get over it? I can't believe you. If he really cared about us, he would be here. Not making drop by visits when the thought crosses his mind. When he does show up, he acts like he's running things over here.

He ain't the man of this house, I am. We don't need him. I'm going to take care of you and Ma."

"Let's be clear..." Jalen's mother interrupted. "I run things in this house."

"I know, Ma. I'm just sayin'."

Jalen's father had left his family because he didn't want the responsibility. It was easier for him to lay up with other women in their Section 8 housing and throw a few dollars their way to help with the five and six kids they had, rather than be a father to his own kids. Jalen had no respect for him. He could have had another family and they wouldn't have known.

"I appreciate you being the man of the house and all but I won't need you or anybody else to take care of me. After I get my degree, I'll be paid."

"I hear you talking but let me enlighten you, Ms. Degree. Over one billion people go to college, with that same ambition in mind, but how many of them do you think really make it? The real world isn't conducted in the classroom. Success isn't based on a class agenda, so don't count your paper just yet. The word on the street is a college degree trade-in is only worth a donut and a twenty-ounce cup of coffee these days, so watch yourself."

"No, you watch yourself. And I'm not thinking about no word on the street. I have what I consider to be a reasonable expectation of life. What kinds of expectations do you have other than getting high on crack pipe dreams? Maybe one day you'll wake up and realize that this tape recorder lifestyle you're living can't be put

8

on pause or rewind, while you go through life on fast forward, getting into whatever dirt you can find to get into next. So while you're at it, go bite that donut."

Raquel rolled her eyes at her brother and gave her mother a high five slap on her palm. The two women laughed but Jalen didn't find her funny. He walked out of the kitchen, leaving them at the table and letting her have the last word. Who was she to criticize him? She didn't know what his dreams were. Just because he didn't talk to her about them didn't mean he didn't have any. Jalen felt like his sister was a naïve schoolgirl. She was living in a fantasy world. She had no idea what the world was like, but he did. He let them make fun of him, tell him he wouldn't amount to anything because they didn't have a clue about the money he could make and the connections he had, even if they were criminal connections. He went to his room and pulled out some shorts to play ball in. He would always be there for his sister but some lessons she would have to learn on her own. Right now, he was going to teach Cantalope some lessons in basketball.

Cantalope had mad skills in basketball. He could have gone pro if it weren't for the huge obstacle in his way, school. He knew that regardless of his skills, he didn't have a chance because school was a requirement in order to get into any kind of organized ball. Cantalope and Jalen were both fourteen. Their lives were similar but very different. Neither of them had a positive male figure in their lives. Jalen's father had walked away but Cantalope was ten when his father died, after which he was never the same. He could be withdrawn and defensive, always ready for a fight. His demeanor was like there was nothing in his life that mattered, except Jalen. Cantalope didn't have any dreams of his own, so he lived vicariously through Jalen. Instead of dreams, his mind was clouded with anger and pessimism.

Jalen and Cantalope hit the court. Yells came at Jalen and Cantalope from the other guys that were already putting together their squads. Everybody knew that if you wanted to win, you needed Jalen and Cantalope on your team and you had to have both because they only played together.

"I got Jay and Lope," one guy yelled.

Jalen and Cantalope stood to the side checking out who was on the court. They wanted to pick their own squad.

11

"What, y'all holdin' out? Y'all niggas too good to play on somebody else's squad?" yelled Terrell.

Terrell was a neighborhood big mouth who complained about everything. He was a six-foot, two-hundred-pound crybaby.

"We too good to play with you, punk. Now what? You just mad you can't play ball the way you run your mouth," said Cantalope.

"I'm just saying, all these niggas out here hollerin' for you to be on their team. Like y'all the dream team or some shit."

"Fuck you!" Cantalope said, walking towards Terrell.

Terrell mumbled something under his breath. Cantalope didn't know what he said and it really didn't matter. He had heard enough.

"What you say? Bitch ass nigga. Always whining about something."

Cantalope was in his face, waiting for him to make a move. If Terrell mumbled anything, he was going to hit him. Jalen pulled Cantalope away from Terrell. He knew what was about to happen, that once Lope reached a certain point it was over, and it didn't take much to get to that point.

"Come on, Lope, man we ain't trying to go there. I thought we were here to run this ball," said Jalen.

The other guy's on the court stood back and watched. They all knew Cantalope had a short fuse.

"Whatever, J. This dude act like he got something to get off of his chest. I'm just trying to help him out."

"Come on, man," Jalen pleaded.

Cantalope finally backed away from Terrell and put his hands out for Jalen to pass him the ball.

"Are we gon' play or what?"

Crime Paid

What comes out of a man is what makes him unclean. For from within, **out of men's hearts**, come evil thoughts, sexual immorality, theft, murder, adultery, greed, malice, deceit, lewdness, envy, slander, arrogance and folly.

Mark 7:22

"Reggie pass that shit."

"A'ight nigga, damn." Reggie took another hit then passed the joint to his left.

"Jay, man how long you been smokin'?" asked Reggie.

"Man, I started when I was eleven years old."

"Eleven years old?" Donald echoed, in disbelief.

"Uh, yeah eleven years old. What, you a fuckin' mockin' bird?"

"Naw, you just caught me off guard with that one. I mean, yo momma wasn't even letting you walk to school by yourself at eleven, was she?" Donald laughed then took a hit.

"Go 'head with that," Jay countered, laid back in his chair waiting for his turn to come back around.

The four teenagers sat with their chairs in a circle passing a joint that Reggie had rolled. Reggie was eighteen years old, two years older than the other boys were. He was from a large family of brothers and sisters that were on either drugs or selling them. Donald was homeless. He stayed at different people's houses from day to day. His father died when he was very young and he never talked about his mother. Sometimes he would stay at Cantalopes' house for months at a time. I think he thought that if he just kept telling jokes, no one would realize that he was damn near living with them just not paying rent. He dropped out of school in the sixth grade and

never seemed to care about going back.
Sam was born a troublemaker. Whenever
there was trouble in the neighborhood, more
than likely Sam was involved. He was
always getting caught by the police for
something. With his luck, he was sure to be
a drop out just like Donald. Sam hardly ever
went to school and when he did, he ended up
getting expelled. They all lived in Tolliver
Court, an apartment complex in Capital
Heights. The neighborhood was drug
infested and the police stayed on call. The
neighbors knew each other, and were on a
first name basis, but if your car got stolen,
you'd be hard pressed for a witness. They
were, for the most part, hard working people
who didn't want any trouble.

"What about you, Donald?" asked
Jalen.

"I'm not sure, but I know it wasn't eleven."

"Whatever, nigga," Jay snorted, then took another hit.

"What about you, Reg.? When did you start smoking?" asked Jalen.

"Whatever, nigga, if I recall you the one that got me started smoking two years ago, one day when we stayed home from school."

"Oh yeah, that's right. You can thank me later," said Jalen, laughing. "Yo ass was tow up from the flo' up."

"Jay, back to you. What got you smokin' weed at eleven?" asked Donald.

"One night, my cousin Bird stayed at our house. We were out on the balcony rolling up a joint. I don't know where Momma was but I thought he was about to smoke a cigarette so I asked him what was

he doing? He told me to come here and shut
the door. Said he had something he wanted
me to try. He said I couldn't tell anybody,
not even Cantalope. I said 'yeah, okay.'
I've been smoking ever since. That shit they
be talking about on TV, 'This is your brain
on drugs.' Then they fry a egg, is some
bullshit. It haven't done shit to me. All I do
is laugh all day and eat junk food. As long
as I keep my mints, my Visene and my
Lagerfeld in my pocket, it's business as
usual. Pass the joint …"

"Jay, here comes your cousin, late as
usual. Man, why is your peoples always late
for everything? We said that we were going
to meet out here an hour ago. That nigga
always the last one to get here," said Reggie,
exhaling smoke.

"That's Lope. Just let it go."

Cantalope walked into the empty laundry room, of the abandoned building, that the boys had designated as their meeting place. Their meetings were usually just to smoke weed, make plans on who to rob next, or just to hang out. Cantalope did a what's up head nod to everybody.

"What's up, fellas?"

"What's up, Lope?" Reggie was the first to answer.

"What's up, Reg? I see you negros couldn't wait for a brotha before y'all started firing up joints, huh?"

"Wait for a brotha? Boy we gon' be waitin' for you at your funeral. Here you go, you know we saved you some," Donald teased, passing Cantalope the joint.

"My man."

Cantalope took a few hits while the meeting got started. The real reason they were meeting up.

"So what's up, cousin? Are you rolling with us tonight or what?"

"Jay, y'all niggas are talking about robbing the sporting goods store?"

"Yeah, you in or what?"

"I'm down. Who else is going to make sure this thing is ran smoothly?" asked Cantalope.

This wasn't the first time the group had burglarized a store. They had hit other smaller stores in the past two years, always avoiding being caught. They had guidelines, a sort of rulebook. One of the most important rules was time. They would watch each spot for at least thirty days prior to robbing it. That was the rule.

The robbery went as planned. As usual, Donald was nervous, Reggie wandered away from everyone else, and Cantalope followed behind Jalen, down for whatever. The boys executed their plan with precision. They made it out of the store with over three thousand dollars worth of sports and winter gear. They held a Tolliver Court-style sidewalk sale and each boy walked away with five hundred dollars in his pocket, not a bad cut for eight minutes of work.

Jalen's mentality and appetite for crime had increased, burglarizing homes without the others. Every break-in made him feel more invincible. He studied his target and planned each robbery to perfection. He felt like no one could touch him. The others didn't have his intuition.

"Jay, wake up," Cantalope whispered.

Jalen squinted his eyes trying to see his cousin in the dark.

"What's up?"

"The guys are outside. We gon' go back to the school."

Jalen laid with his eyes closed, thinking about what his cousin was saying to him.

"I'm not messin' with it. I have a bad feeling about this one. Y'all need to think this through. How you just gon' rush into this without a plan."

"Yeah I know but the fellas are all outside and we have all of the tools so we're gonna just run in and out. It shouldn't be any different from the last time."

"I ain't feelin' this one, cuz. You shouldn't go tonight."

"OK well you sit this one out, and as soon as we get back I will come and get you so that we can show you what we got."

"I'm tryin' to tell you, I don't feel good about it."

"I feel you. I'll holla at you when we get back."

Jalen let his cousin leave but he had a bad feeling that the night wasn't going to turn out the way Cantalope and the other boys expected.

Cantalope, Reggie, Donald and Sam left for the school. As they walked through the woods, taking the shortcut to the school, Cantalope didn't share Jalen's feeling with the other boys. He just told them Jalen was tired and they would get up with him later. He left Jalen's feeling confident. They agreed to stay true to their eight-minute rule.

However, this time, eight minutes wasn't enough. They didn't know the school had just installed a silent alarm. The police were there in four minutes. Sam got caught because he was trying too hard to be an engineer. When the police entered the school, he was upstairs in the mechanical room studying the cable schematics of the building. Reggie thought he was home free, running out of the fire emergency door. The sound of the fire alarm was piercing but it didn't distract him. To his surprise, the police were standing outside of the door waiting for him. Cantalope decided he would not be caught that easily. He put up a fight. One of the cops decided to release the dog on him.

"Get him, Hero."

The German Sheppard jumped on Cantalope and attacked him, leaving a huge chunk of meat hanging from his arm. Cantalope wasn't going to let the dog get the best of him. He grabbed the dog by the mouth and bit him in the face, sending "Hero" running like the dog he was. Cantalope didn't realize he had just assaulted an officer. The Police beat Cantalope leaving him with eighty-five stitches before dropping him at Boys Village for the next three days. Donald was the only one who got away. When the police ran into the school, he slipped out quietly.

Donald went to Jalen and told him what had happened to Cantalope. Jalen stood outside talking to Donald, mad that he couldn't do anything to help his cousin and even more mad that he hadn't listened to him in the first place. Fear for his own freedom gripped him.

"I hope them niggas don't start runnin' off at the mouth about any of the other shit we did."

"Come on, man. You know Lope wouldn't say nothin', especially not about you."

"I know not Lope but what about Sam and Reggie?"

"You know better. They cool."

Jalen had been robbing stores on his own and not telling the other boys. But what was to stop them from telling about the other robberies. Donald's words weren't totally reassuring but Jalen knew there wasn't anything else he could do but wait.

After a few weeks had gone by, and Jalen was able to talk to Cantalope, he felt

more at ease that no one had snitched. He
resumed his crime spree, alone. He
continued meeting with his friends at their
meeting place, smoked weed with them, and
shot ball with them, but any plans he had of
burglarizing stores he kept to himself.
Jalen's mother finally moved them out of
Capital Heights. He seemed to lose his
enthusiasm for stealing but not for money.
He had made some good money robbing
stores but after Big Moe put him on to the
drug game, Jalen knew what it was to make
money. Big Moe lived on Georgia Avenue.
Jalen had met him at a go-go at the Ibex. He
introduced Jalen to cocaine. It wasn't long
before he was making so much money
hustling cocaine and love boat that school
was like a part-time job that he hated going
to. Jalen started skipping school or going

late. He was failing but none of it matter.
All that mattered to him was making money.
The drawback was not being able to spend
his money the way he really wanted. There
was no lie he could tell his mother that
would explain the thousands of dollars a
week that he was bringing home. As Jalen
perfected his craft, dropping major product
with his runners weekly, he kept up his
charade.

"What's up, J?"

"Nothin much."

"Jalen, call me later."

Jalen followed his regular morning
routine. He would get off the school bus at
the back entrance with everybody else then
walk straight down the hall and out the front
door to the 7-11 down the street from the
school. He bought his usual breakfast, a

donut and orange juice. Jalen decided to roll a joint of the boat he had wet down earlier that morning. It usually took about four hours for the weed to dry but he didn't have that kind of time this morning. He didn't get started until 4:30 a.m. and it was only 8:00.

"Let's see if this shit is right."

Jalen rolled the joint and then fired it up. He sucked on the small cigarette and then exhaled after holding it for a few seconds. After another couple of puffs, he could feel the drug taking affect.

"Damn, this is some good shit."

Jalen was pleased with his product and decided it was ready to deliver to his runners. School didn't mean much to him but he tried to do just enough not to get put out so he decided to make his delivery at lunchtime. Hopefully no one would smell the drugs in his locker before then. Jalen put his hand to his mouth to take another hit. He stood up and threw his backpack on his back. Before he could exhale, his body hit the ground.

Jalen could hear people moving around him. He heard monitors beeping and someone yelling, "I think we're losing him." He tried to open his eyes to look around but everything was a blur.

Jalen tried to speak but nothing came out. A tube was inserted in his nose and run down his throat. He found out later that the tube in his throat was used to pump his stomach.

"Get that I.V. going. I think he's going to be alright."

Jalen opened his eyes and saw his mother sitting at his bedside, wiping her eyes. His sister sat in a nearby chair with her head back and her eyes closed, taking a nap.

"Ma, what happened?" asked Jalen.

Raquel sat up and opened her eyes.

"Oh you're awake," said Raquel.

"What happened?"

"I'll tell you what happened. You scared us half to death. You overdosed!" shouted Raquel.

"Jalen I had no idea. How long has this been going on? I thought that by moving I was getting you away from that kind of element. How in the world did you get hooked up with drugs?"

Jalen suddenly felt ashamed. What was he supposed to tell his mother? How could he explain an accidental drug overdose?

"What are you some kind of big time drug dealer? The police said the drugs they found in your bag would have been worth thousands of dollars on the street."

"Damn, the police," Jalen said, putting his head back against the pillow wondering how much worse things would get, especially if the police had his bag.

"Jalen, I work hard every day trying to provide for you and your sister. Why would you sell drugs?"

Jalen was quiet. He didn't know how to tell his mother that he could make more in a week than she made in a whole month. His shame forced him to say nothing. He knew he had let her down, the one thing he never wanted to do. He wanted his mother to be proud of him and talk highly of him the way she did about his sister. Even if he told her how much money he made on the streets, she wouldn't be proud. He knew that, but the fast money and the drugs had him.

"Mrs. Gibson? My name is Doctor Willis. I'm here to talk to Jalen."

A tall black man in a business suit interrupted them.

"I thought Doctor Preston was his doctor?" asked Jalen's mother.

"He is his medical doctor. I am a psychiatrist. When you are treated for an overdose, the hospital will not release you until you have talked to a psychiatrist."

"I don't need a psychiatrist. I didn't try to kill myself," argued Jalen.

"You may not have intentionally overdosed but using illegal drugs is a form of unconscious self destruction."

"What are you talking about? I just smoked a joint before it was ready to be smoked."

For a second he forgot that his mother was in the room. She looked at him with sadness and disappointment. Jalen turned his head away from her and the doctor, and looked out the window.

"Mrs. Gibson, I'd like to speak to Jalen alone."

Jalen's mother and sister left the room.

"Jalen, I understand that this was an accident but you need to understand that drugs are a problem. You were lucky this time. The next time you might not be so lucky."

"There won't be a next time. I know what I did wrong."

The doctor looked at Jalen. He knew he wasn't getting through to the boy.

"What did you do wrong?"

"I smoked that shit before it was completely dry."

"Do you realize what you are doing to your body? You don't realize it but there is a bigger underlying problem that you are hiding."

"Hiding?"

"Yes hiding. Drugs are only a temporary escape from a bigger problem."

"Man, look, you said I had to talk to you before the hospital will release me. Well I've talked to you. I'm done."

Jalen turned his head and looked out the window, indicating that he was finished with the conversation. The doctor didn't press.

"I am going to recommend that you attend a drug treatment program."

The doctor scribbled on the chart that hung on the front of Jalen's hospital bed, then left the room. Jalen knew that the doctor was trying to help him but right now, he didn't want to hear what he had to say. After he got home from the hospital, he laid in his bed, looking at the ceiling, thinking how crime had paid. Now he was embarrassed and humiliated. Not only did his mother know about him using and selling drugs, and return to school to face his schoolmates, some of whom looked up to him, but at some point he was going to have to deal with the police. He closed his eyes and prayed. He hadn't talked to God in a long time. God was no stranger to Jalen. They used to go to church as a family every

Sunday before his father left. After a while, his mother started working so much that she was too tired to get up and go to church on Sunday. It had been a long time but Jalen knew how to pray. He closed his eyes and talked quietly to God, promising to do better and to be a better person if God would help him out of this mess. When he finished pleading his case, he turned over and went to sleep. There was nothing else he could do but wait to see if God would answer him. He hoped there was still enough grace for God to show him some mercy.

Apparently, God heard Jalen's prayer. The police had dropped the drug charges against him. The backpack full of drugs that Jalen had been carrying when he passed out was missing. It was lost somewhere in the evidence room. Jalen couldn't believe it

when his lawyer called to say the charges
had been dropped. However, he didn't have
the same luck with the Prince George's
County School Board. He was not allowed
to return to school until after he completed a
licensed drug rehabilitation program. His
mother put him on her version of house
arrest and he wasn't allowed to go anywhere
but the clinic for six months. Jalen thought
he would go crazy with cabin fever but
when it was all over, he finally had a
different outlook on life. He had survived a
drug over dose, lucked up and missed a
possible jail sentence, and through drug
rehab, he was getting his life back. He had
one more hurdle to jump before it was all
over. He had to graduate from high school.
To make things worse he had to return to the
scene of the crime. Jalen's mother made

him go back to Suitland High School. She told him if he had been bad enough to smoke drugs and sell drugs then he was bad enough to go back there and do whatever it took to graduate.

After repeating the ninth and tenth grades because selling drugs was more important than school, returning back to school after his accidental overdose and rehabilitation, Jalen finally graduated in 1988 with honors after going to summer school for ten hours a day. Less than thirty days after graduation, he was on a plane to boot camp. Jalen looked out the window of the airplane as it left BWI airport. He was on his way to a new life and a new beginning, leaving behind a childhood of misdeeds. His cousin, and best friend Cantalope, was sentenced to twenty years for murder. He had seen so many of his friends killed or in jail. Jalen remembered his prayer to God, asking for help out of the life he was living. He believed God had answered his call. The United States Army was his way out.

Getting Out

Be careful **never to forget** what you yourself have seen. Do not let these memories escape from your mind as long as you live!

Deuteronomy 4:9

Jalen got off the bus at Ft. Leonard Wood, Missouri. He had no idea what boot camp was going to be like but he was ready for anything. His childhood had been full of crime, drugs, and regret, but he had overcome it all. He had finally made a decision to change his life and it was going to start right here. Jalen was determined to make his mother proud. She continued to support him no matter what he did. The things she knew about were just the tip of the iceberg. If he could help it, she would never know the whole story. She would never know how involved he was with drugs, or how many houses or schools or people he had robbed. She didn't need to know about those things. All she needed to know was that she had a son that made her proud, and this is where it would happen.

Boot camp was a breeze for Jalen. He worked hard and excelled in all his tests, both the physical and the written. He was a favorite among his superiors. After being called on to give the cadence, Jalen decided to write a few cadence of his own. His drill Sergeant was impressed and decided to use them. Later it won him the Drill Sergeant of the Cycle Award. Jalen mastered the art of impressing his superiors.

After boot camp, Jalen was stationed with the 9th Engineer Battalion in West Germany. Making new friends had never been a problem for Jalen, but he was especially surprised to find that he had friends in Germany before he even got there. He and two other privates, fresh out of boot camp, stood at attention while the 1st Sergeant looked over their orders.

"Private Bryant."

"Yes, sir?"

"Boy, I work for a living. Don't call me sir, you can call me TOP."

"Yes 1st Sergeant, I mean TOP."

"You won't be in this company. You'll be in Charlie Company. I only have room for two."

"Yes 1st Sergeant."

Before the Sergeant could finish with Private Bryant, the door to his office swung open.

"Clark, what the hell are you doing?" barked the Sergeant.

"Sorry TOP, but I heard I got a homeboy in here. Which one of y'all dudes is from DC?" asked Private Clark.

"I'm from Chi-town," Private Haynes responded.

"Well then I'm not talking to you. My man, how 'bout you? You from DC?" Private Clark asked, questioning Jalen.

"Yeah I'm from DC," said Jalen.

"TOP, you gotta put him in my room."

"Clark, get the hell outta my office."

"Come on, TOP. He's my homeboy."

"Clark!"

The 1st Sergeant gave the private a look and he left without another word. After he finished briefing the two privates, he sent Jalen to room with Specialist Clark, Stephen. The two hit it off just as Stephen knew they would. He enjoyed having someone from his hometown so close. It was like having a little piece of home. Jalen was glad Stephen had befriended him. He was determined to make a change in his life but decided it wouldn't hurt to have a friend to help him along the way.

It didn't take Jalen long to fool the Army into thinking he was some extraordinary kind of guy just as he had in boot camp. He was a favorite among his superiors. The spotlight was no longer on him because he was the top dog selling drugs in the hood. He was quickly becoming top dog in his battalion.

"Privates Gibson and Clark?" called Sergeant Johnson.

"Yes, sir?"

Stephen and Jalen stood at attention when the Sergeant stepped into their tent. He had been standing on the outside of the tent listening to their conversation about how, among other things, white men couldn't dunk. Sergeant Johnson was a white, over eager, army man who didn't particularly care for the black soldiers.

"I had the privilege of overhearing some of your thought-provoking conversation on the differences between whites and blacks."

Stephen was nervous, afraid of what Sergeant Johnson was planning. Jalen stood at attention not at all concerned with Sergeant Johnson or his intentions.

"I say, let's put this theory of yours to the test. Follow me."

Jalen and Stephen followed the Sergeant out of the tent.

"You see that mountain over there?" the Sergeant asked, pointing in the direction of what looked like the tallest mountain in Wildflicken. "A race to the top of the mountain. You two and another black soldier of your choice against me, and two white soldiers of my choice. And to make it even more interesting I'll throw in twenty dollars, plus my meals for the week."

"Sure, we'll take that bet," said Jalen.

Stephen looked at Jalen in disbelief. The Sergeant saw Stephen's look and decided to press the competition even further.

"Oh, I forgot to mention you have to carry a sixty-caliber rifle up the mountain with you to disassemble then reassemble before you start back down the mountain. Your group only wins if all of you make it back down before every member of my group."

Stephen looked at Jalen, who had never flinched, and saw that his friend was serious about the challenge.

"When do we do it?" asked Stephen.

Jalen and Stephen recruited Sergeant Lewis, a black Sergeant that looked like the character from Fat Albert's gang with the hubba-bubba lips. Sergeant Johnson picked two white soldiers to be on his team, Specialist Kyle Newton, who was a known KKK supporter, and Sergeant Josh Hampton. Sergeant Hampton couldn't stand Jalen and Jalen had no idea why. The six men started up the mountain with their weapons following closely behind one another. Each man kept up with his white counterpart. After two hours, they finally reached the top of the mountain. Although they all reached the top at the same time,

Jalen, Stephen, and Sergeant Lewis disassembled then reassembled their weapons in record time and were on their way back down the mountain. Stephen and Sergeant Lewis crossed the finish line and turned to check Jalen's progress. He wasn't far behind. Jalen jogged into the finish line, not concerned with the competition, because they weren't in his peripheral vision. He wasn't so pressed about the twenty dollars or the meals. His focus was on beating Sergeant Johnson and making the others look like fools. Stephen and Sergeant Lewis cheered Jalen on to the finish line. Just as Jalen crossed the finish line, Colonel Jimeola, the top Colonel of the Battalion, walked out of a tent.

"Private Gibson? How are you?"

Jalen had met the Colonel during a Battalion room inspection. The Colonel saw all of Jalen's go-go pictures on the wall and called it a shrine. Jalen joked around with the Colonel while everyone else stood back scared to talk to him because of his rank. The Colonel never forgot Jalen.

Jalen immediately stood at attention and saluted Colonel Jimeola.

"Fine, Colonel Jimeola, sir."

"What's going on here?"

Also, Colonel Jimeola had given him the Commanding General's Award—an award given to soldiers who excelled in all areas of training—while he was in boot camp. When the Colonel presented it to him, he told him he was the first African American ever to receive that award.

The Colonel decided to present Jalen with the Battalion coin. It was his second. Most soldiers never got one and those that did, the Colonel didn't call them all by name. Jalen had them all thinking he was the best soldier the army ever had. Stephen couldn't believe it. He just shook his head. He was used to his friend getting attention from the higher ranked officers. Jalen worked his way up to Specialist before he completed his four years. He had traveled around the world for the army. He had taught other soldiers how to disarm land mines, and he felt lucky not to be coming home in a body bag like other members of his battalion that he had served with in Desert Storm. That whole experience had blown his mind. One more time, he felt like his friends were being taken away from him, like his childhood friend Reggie, who was caught trying to rob a bank and sentenced to twenty-five years for armed robbery. His best friend and cousin, Cantalope, was also doing hard time in jail and no one knew when or if he would ever get out. He even missed the thought of Donald just hanging around. The police found Donald dead from an overdose in an abandoned building.

When Jalen returned to the United States from Germany, he was stationed in Kansas, where he met the woman that opened his eyes to a whole other side of sex. Up to now, Jalen had slept with a hand full of women but sex was never a big deal to him. If it didn't involve money, it wasn't at the top of his priority list. Melanie was five-foot-five inches, brown skinned with hazel brown eyes and a soft voice, and big pretty breasts. Jalen loved a woman with big breasts. When Jalen set his eyes on her in the PX on base, he knew he had to have her, for the night anyway. He sweet-talked her into going out with him. Afterwards he took her home and it was on. Melanie was a southern girl from Atlanta and she was all about pleasing her man. She was the first woman to ever suck his dick and make him have an orgasm. When she touched him, his whole body tingled. He had never been with a woman like her before. When Melanie was done with him, he felt like he finally knew what it was to make love to a woman, or more accurately, what it felt like to have a woman make love to him. Sex, with his on again off again high school girlfriend, was okay but this woman knew what it meant to please her man. Jalen laid back on the pillows and watched her every move. She squirmed and moaned while she sucked on his head and stroked his shaft. When he finally came, she swallowed every drop and came right along with him. Jalen's mind was blown. He had never seen a woman have an orgasm just from giving head. That night he felt like he was the woman and she was the man. She was in total control. After he came, she kept sucking his dick until it got hard again. Then she straddled him and slid down on him. Moving her hips back and forth, moaning, Jalen grabbed her hips and lifted her up and down. She held onto his chest and pounded against him. Jalen was surprised by the sounds she made. She was really enjoying him. He knew he was no slouch in bed but he had no idea he could have this type of affect on a woman.

When he flipped her over and pounded her from behind, she cried out.

"Baby, I'm coming."

And she kept on coming. Jalen had never experienced a woman having multiple orgasms. His lovemaking was so good that Melanie asked Jalen to move in a week later. She bought him clothes and jewelry just to keep him happy so that he wouldn't leave but, when his tour was up, Jalen decided it was time to go home. Melanie was heartbroken. Jalen was confused. He had enjoyed their sexship but that's all that it was, sex. She cried and offered to give him anything he wanted if he would stay. He didn't change his mind but this whole situation with Melanie got him to thinking. Women walked around all the time pimping men, withholding sex for money, clothes, and anything else they could get. Jalen had no intention of going back on the streets and selling drugs to make his money. He was now a responsible adult, but there were other ways to make money. If Melanie was willing to spend her money on him, he wondered what other women would do for sex. He returned to Maryland with a new look on life, making money, and women.

Drink Up

But by the grace of God, I am **what I am**, and His grace to me was not without effect.

1 Corinthians 15:10

Jalen had left Melanie in Kansas because he missed home. Kansas was quiet and peaceful. He missed the hustle of DC, and the fine women of Chocolate City. Melanie was a sweet country girl with a big heart. Jalen was ready for a challenge. He wanted to see just how good he really was with women and how much they were willing to pay. To his surprise, it was easier than he'd thought. All he had to do was listen to their problems as if he cared, pay attention to the little things, and screw their brains out. Jalen's cell phone rang constantly. He never considered himself to have a big penis but it did the job. Two months after being home, he had a fully furnished apartment, with the rent paid every month, a brand new truck, and money in his pocket; kept by the women that he slept with. His mind was like a daily planner, each woman having a separate file. Jalen was able to keep them separate and under control. They had to follow his rules or he would stop seeing them and never talk to them again. No one wanted to be ignored by Jalen so they all followed his rules. Everyone except LaShawn.

LaShawn was married with two children but that didn't stop her from giving Jalen anything he wanted, whenever he wanted. She had paid his rent for months at a time, while giving him all or part of his truck note. She always checked his refrigerator to make sure he had food and if need be she would go to the grocery store for him. Jalen thought she was perfect until she showed him another side to her. When he didn't answer her calls, she started showing up at his apartment banging on the door. When he wouldn't answer the door, she would sit in front of his building blowing the horn to get his attention. One morning, as he was leaving for work, he found four flat tires. The time after that, it was a broken windshield. Repeatedly, he broke it off with her but each time she would draw him back in. LaShawn gave him what none of the other women would. She had ass for days and she loved anal sex. Jalen took everything she gave him but because there were five other women giving him money, at any given moment, he stopped asking her for money. Instead, he asked her to pay his cell phone bill. LaShawn agreed but she insisted on buying him a new phone. The one he had was over a year old and she wanted him to have a new one if she was going to pay the bill. Jalen agreed without considering the fact that she would have access to his bills because the phone was in her name. This mistake would cost him more than he bargained for.

LaShawn paced the kitchen floor, waiting for the last woman to arrive. She was surprised the other women had shown up. After going through Jalen's phone records and seeing the same numbers repeatedly at two and three in the morning, she decided to call them. Nothing could have prepared her for what would happen afterward. Every number belonged to a different woman. When the first woman answered, LaShawn let her know that Jalen was her man and that she paid the bill on his cell phone. The woman responded very calmly explaining to LaShawn that it was best for her to talk to Jalen and not to call her again. She didn't stop until she had called every number on the bill. Some of the numbers were just buddies of his but most of them belonged to women. Instead of cursing at each woman, LaShawn decided to talk to the women and find out just how involved they were with Jalen. Twenty calls later, and a night of crying her eyes out, LaShawn decided she wanted to meet them. She wanted to see what the other women looked like and why Jalen had cheated on her.

When Gale knocked on the door, she could hear what sounded like a lot of people inside. Her cousin Cheryl had called and asked her to meet her. With all of the noise, she assumed it was some kind of party.

"Hi is Cheryl here?" Gale asked, when the door finally opened.

"Come one in," said LaShawn, holding the door open for Gale to enter. "Go on into the living room. Everyone else is already here."

"I'm just here because my cousin called and told me to come over. What's going on? It sounds like a party," Gale said, walking into the living room where the other women were.

Gale looked around the room for her cousin Cheryl. She finally spotted her sitting on the other side of the room. Gale sat in the empty chair next to Cheryl.

"What's going on?"

Before Cheryl could answer, Gale noticed someone else in the room that she recognized.

"Hey Nina!. How you doin'? I haven't seen you in a long time."

Nina didn't answer, looking from Gale to Cheryl, waiting for Cheryl to tell Gale what the meeting was all about. LaShawn found her seat and introduced Gale to everyone.

"Gale, my name is LaShawn. That is Juanita, Terri, Amina, Traneida, Veronica, and Janice. I know this is a fucked up way to find out but we are all sleeping with the same man. Jalen Gibson," LaShawn said, pointing to each of the women in the room.

"What? What are you talking about? Cheryl, what's going on?"

"She's right. Jalen is fucking or has fucked every woman in this room," Cheryl confirmed.

Gale looked at her cousin confused.

"How did you find out? Why are you here?"

"LaShawn called Nina and after they talked Nina called me and told me about LaShawn and the other women. I told her hell yeah she needed to show up and meet these other women. I called you here because you needed to know too."

"Wait a minute. Nina, you're fucking Jalen? How could you do something like that? I thought we were friends, and Cheryl, you are my cousin, how could you not tell me?"

"Because I'm your cousin and Nina is my best friend. I didn't want your feelings

68

to be hurt. You think Jalen is the best thing to ever happen to you. I was willing to let it slide, the fact that he had slept with Nina, until now."

"Let it slide?" Gale looked at her cousin with disgust. Then she walked over to Nina. "You dirty bitch."

Nina stood up and the two women were face to face.

"Gale, I'm sorry I was wrong but Jalen is the problem not me."

"Jalen? What about you? You nasty bitch."

"I know you're upset but I'm not going to be anymore of your bitches. It's your own fault."

Cheryl stood between the two women and tried to calm her cousin.

"Gale, come on. He's not worth it."

Gale ignored her cousin and addressed Nina's statement instead.

"What do you mean it's my fault?"

"Gale, sit down," Cheryl instructed, pushing her gently back to her seat.

Gale sat down and waited for Nina to explain. Nina was a thirty-five-year-old white woman that only stood five-foot-two. She and Gale had gone to college together. Before Jalen, Nina never had any interest in black men.

"All you used to talk about was how big Jalen's dick was and how you wished you could get it everyday. I would usually just ignore you but one night I caught a ride home with y'all. I got out of class before you did so Jalen and I were sitting in the car talking, waiting for you. We got into a conversation about relationships and sex. I made a comment about men being led by their dicks. He started talking about how big his dick was but that he wasn't led by it. He gave me his number and told me to call him and we could talk about it in detail. I did not intend to call him but later on I got to drinking and smoking and before I knew it, we were in his bed. I never meant to hurt you. It was only supposed to be one time but it ended up being every Wednesday at ten o'clock. I didn't mean to but I fell in love with him."

"In love?" Cheryl asked before Gayle had the chance.

"What do you mean in love? You said you slept with him one time."

"What was I going to tell you? I'm in love with your cousin's man. I had no idea about these other women."

"I hate to breakup this little 'Waiting to Exhale' party but I don't want to be a part of this," said Terri.

Terri was a forty-year-old light-skinned woman. She had met Jalen in a sports bar. They started out as friends but eventually became lovers. Terri cherished his friendship and even though she was just as hurt by all of the women in the room she refused to sit by and listen to them tell their stories about Jalen.

"Jay and I had a lot of fun together and now it's over. I've moved on, I suggest you all do the same."

"I agree," said Janice, who also decided to leave.

Janice was a fifty-year-old, green-eyed,
Christian woman, with the least amount of
time invested in Jalen but she felt like she
was all the better for having been involved
with him. Her friends never approved of
Jalen because he was so much younger but
Janice was in love with him. Sleeping with
Jalen was against her beliefs but he made
her feel alive. Abigail was forty-nine,
almost twice Jalen's age and she didn't care
about anything the other women were
saying. She didn't care what Jalen did as
long as he told her he loved her when he was
with her. She had heard enough and decided
to leave with the other two women.
Traneida also decided to leave. Traneida
was forty and couldn't imagine her life
without Jalen. She had fallen so hard for

him that she walked away from a four-year relationship, leaving her fiancé at the altar.

As the women exited the room and then out the front door, Juanita began her story of how she and Jalen met. Juanita was a forty-five-year-old, single mother, with plenty of money in the bank that she didn't mind giving to Jalen.

"About four months after I met Jalen, I made it clear to him that he could get it. I slept with him thinking it was only going to be one time but that was just the beginning. I was like his puppet. Anything he wanted I was willing to give him. It got to the point where I was paying him for sex. I was paying him three hundred dollars a week to give him oral sex and, in return, he gave me the biggest orgasms I've ever had. Over the course of three years, I'm sure I had given him well over twenty-five thousand dollars to sleep with me once a week."

Juanita paused, dropping her head and playing with her hands.

"I feel like a fool," she said, almost in tears. "I paid for his apartment, his truck, and his clothes. I would beg him to go on vacations with me and then give him spending money after we got there. All I wanted was for him to make love to me a couple of nights a week. Make me feel like a real woman, like I was alive."

"Honey, don't feel like a fool," Veronica interrupted. "Jalen has a way of getting you hooked and reeling you in. Even when you know that he's baiting you, you still go for it. I did. I knew Jalen was a playa the first time I met him five years ago. We worked together for a while, part-time.

He was always on the telephone or smiling in some woman's face. I have to admit, I was curious so I baited him to see what he would do. To my surprise, he was a complete gentleman. We had good conversation and he was funny. I was lonely and I needed some laughter in my life. For months, we did nothing but talk. Then I started to wonder about myself. Wasn't I attractive enough for him to throw one of his playa moves on me? I went over his house with every intention of getting him in bed. I played it off like I was just there to hang out with him. He didn't try anything and I chickened out. A week later, I finally asked him why he had never hit on me. He told me to come and see him Monday night, so I did. As soon as I got there, I knew I was making a mistake. Some woman was banging on his window then the door, his cell phone and house phone kept ringing. I should have left but I didn't. He made love to me and I've been with him ever since. I too have given him money and gifts. How much I don't know, but I don't feel bad. He made me feel good and I made him feel good. LaShawn, I don't know what you really wanted to come out of this but I've shared my piece of Jalen and now I'm leaving."

Suddenly there was a light mumbling in the room. Veronica got up to leave and Juanita followed. LaShawn looked at Nina, Cheryl, and Gale. Gale looked sad with tears in her eyes. She and Jalen had been dating for five years and she didn't have a clue. Gale finally got up and walked out. Cheryl and Nina followed. LaShawn was left alone in her living room, with her thoughts of all those other women and Jalen. He had betrayed them all, and made a lot of money while doing it. LaShawn didn't get the chance to tell her story while the other women were there but Jalen had her caught up just like the other women. She thought about how demanding he could be, and his attitude when he didn't get his way. She remembered a time when he had stopped talking to her for a month because he asked her for eleven hundred dollars and she wouldn't give it to him. When it was finally clear that he wasn't going to call, she went to Check-N-Go. They offered loans on the paycheck that you hadn't received yet. She got the money then called to apologize for not giving it to him when he had asked. He took the money and they had make-up sex.

LaShawn decided that Jalen had to pay. She got a glass of wine to help her think. Before the night was over, he would get his.

Jalen looked at the clock on the nightstand. It was 1:15 a.m.

"Who the hell is that?"

He had expected some excitement earlier after he started getting phone calls from all of the women he had been sleeping with. Everybody was upset but nobody had come over. He was glad. He didn't feel like pretending to be sorry for some shit he felt no remorse. They were all grown women. If they felt like they had been taken advantage of, it wasn't his fault. Women were always talking about men using them for their bodies. It felt like to him he was the one being used, whether it was for conversation, a hug, a kiss, or sex. They were all using him in some way. In a way, he was glad they had found out about each other. He needed a break. He finally rolled out of bed to find out who was banging on his door. He looked through the peephole. When he saw that it was LaShawn, he wasn't surprised. She was the crazy one in the bunch. She would bang on his door in the middle of the night if he had told her he didn't want to see her that day. She had slashed his tires and even thrown a cinder block through the window of his truck.

"What do you want, LaShawn? You already cussed me out. I already apologized. What else is there to say?"

"Jay, just let me in for a minute. I want to talk."

"Talk about what? Go home."

"Just give me a few minutes."

Jalen thought about it. His neighbors didn't need a show at one in the morning. He opened the door and let her in.

"Say what you have to say and leave."

"I just wanted to say I forgive you. I talked to those other women and I know they didn't mean anything to you. Since we've been together, I've done some crazy things and you've forgiven me. I want another chance to make this work. All I want is you."

LaShawn walked over to Jalen and rubbed his dick. He was standing in a pair of boxers and a t-shirt. She put her hand on his neck and pulled him close to her. She continued to massage his dick until it was rock hard. Jalen was confused. She had called him every name she could think of on

the telephone and now here she was trying
to make up. Jalen thought about it, it wasn't
confusing. LaShawn was just crazy. He
truly was tired of all the hassle with her and
the other women, and tomorrow he wasn't
going to be bothered with any of them,
money or no money. Tonight he was going
to fuck the shit out of LaShawn. She was
the only one that would let him fuck her in
her ass. She enjoyed it more than he did.
He didn't think there would be anything
wrong with one last time.

When Jalen touched LaShawn, it took
everything in her to remember the real
reason she was there. He pulled her on top
of him and guided her hips back and forth
on his dick. Jalen watched her full breasts
move back and forth with the rhythm of her
hips. He squeezed her hips and smacked her

ass. He watched her breasts jump up and down while he gripped her hips, lifting her up and down on his dick. With every pound, she moaned and he smiled knowing she couldn't get enough of him. LaShawn steadied herself, using Jalen's chest as support. She pounded against him trying to feel him even deeper in her than she already did. Like large rain drops, sweat dripped from her chocolate nipples. Jalen pulled her to him and sucked hard on them.

"Get your ass up and turn around," Jalen commanded.

Panting for air, LaShawn dismounted him and assumed the position. Doggy style was her favorite position, especially when he fucked her in her ass. Jalen played between her legs until his hand was soaked with her juices. He slowly slid his head inside her. He didn't go in her ass, which was what she really wanted, but any hole he chose was fine with her, as long as he was fucking her. Jalen pressed the small of her back, signaling for her to put her head on the bed so that he could go deeper. Her ass cheeks spread wide, slapping loudly against Jalen's abdomen, as he stroked in and out. He pushed deeper and deeper until he felt himself exploding inside her. He groaned, holding on to her so that he wouldn't lose his balance. Before he lost his erection, he pulled his dick out of her and stuck it in her ass. LaShawn stiffened her back, shocked that he was going to give her what he knew she wanted. It didn't take long for her to scream out and cum all over the sheets. Jalen knew her body. He knew she was so excited that he wouldn't have to be in her long before she was cumming everywhere. LaShawn was a squirter. The sheets were soaked with her. Jalen pulled out of her, falling over to the dry side of the bed. They both lay panting and trying to catch their breath. LaShawn felt the heat of being with Jalen finally easing. She rubbed her hand across his sweaty chest then looked down at his dick, her dick. Then she remembered the other women he had fucked repeatedly. Her mouth suddenly felt dirty from the many times she had sucked his dick. She had might as well been eating all of their pussies. She pulled her hand back and turned her head away from him.

"I'm a jump in the shower. You can wash up before you leave, I won't be long."

LaShawn didn't even turn to look at him. They had just made love and he was dismissing her as if she didn't mean a thing to him. She bit her lip hard to keep from going off on him.

"Okay, baby," she said instead.

As soon as LaShawn heard the water from the shower, she hurried to get dressed.

"Baby I poured me a glass of wine. You want one?" LaShawn asked, yelling into the bathroom.

"Yeah that's cool."

After a few minutes, she returned to the bathroom with a glass of wine for Jalen. She had her coat on and her purse on her shoulder.

"I told you, you could wash up. You didn't have to rush out."

"I'm fine. I'll take a shower when I get home. Al isn't home yet."

LaShawn kissed Jalen softly on the lips.

"I'll call you tomorrow," she said, turning and leaving the bathroom.

Jalen thought it was strange that she was leaving so easily, but maybe the night's previous activity had killed some of her fighting spirit. He let her leave without another word. With the towel tied around his waist, he wiped steam from at the bathroom mirror so he could see himself better. He turned his head from side to side, examining his face. He picked up the glass of wine to take a sip. Before he could get the glass to his mouth, he dropped it. The glass broke and wine splattered everywhere.

"Shit!"

LaShawn stood at the front door of the apartment ready to leave. When she heard the glass breaking and Jalen cursing, she smiled.

"Drink up, you bastard."

Finally feeling like she had closure, LaShawn closed the apartment door behind her, finished with Jalen for good.

A Close Call

…you must wander in the wilderness for forty years—a year for each day, suffering the **consequences** of your sins.

Numbers 14:34

"Excuse me. Can you tell me what room Jalen Gibson is in?"

Stephen waited patiently at the information desk, while the woman's fingers danced across the keyboard, looking for the information.

"He was brought into the emergency room and then taken up to the fourth floor, to the cardiac car unit. If you go up there someone should be able to tell you where he is."

"Thanks."

Stephen read the wall signs to get to the elevator. He pushed the button and waited. He couldn't believe his timing. He had called Jalen to let him know he was in town. When Raquel answered Jalen's cell phone and told Stephen that Jay had been taken to the hospital he hung up and jumped in his car. The woman had said the cardiac care unit so Stephen figured it must have been a heart attack. That didn't sound right to him either. Jalen was young, young men didn't have heart attacks. Stephen got off the elevator and walked until he found the nurses desk. There were three nurses working behind the desk. One of the women was on the telephone, another was writing on a patients chart. The male nurse acknowledged Stephen.

"Can I help you?"

"Can you tell me what room Jalen Gibson is in?"

The nurse checked the board for Jalen's name.

"He isn't on the board. Let me check the system."

The male nurse punched a few keys on the keyboard looking for Jalen's name.

"They just put him in a room. You can have a seat in the waiting area and the doctor will come out and let you know when he can have visitors. I think he already has family in the waiting room."

He pointed Stephen in the direction of the waiting room. As soon as he turned the corner, Stephen saw Raquel and Mrs. Gibson, as well as two women he didn't recognize. He had never met Jalen's father but he assumed that the man sitting next to Mrs. Gibson consoling her was Jalen's father.

"Stephen?"

Raquel was the first to notice Stephen in the waiting area.

"Hey, Raquel."

Stephen hugged her as if she was his own sister.

"What's going on with J?"

"We don't know. We've been waiting out here for the doctor to come out."

"What happened? You really didn't say much on the phone."

"J called Momma and told her he thought he was having a heart attack. She was so shook up she couldn't drive. I called 911 and they picked him up and brought him here. We were in the emergency room for three hours before they brought him up here. Now we're just waiting for the doctor."

She stopped, tears suddenly filling her eyes.

"I'm really scared…"

Stephen stopped her before she could finish.

"J is gonna be fine. That nigga ain't goin' nowhere. Your brother doesn't know how to accept defeat."

Stephen hugged Raquel again, walked her over to a chair, and sat down with her.

"And sometimes his crazy butt don't know how to ask for help. I remember one time a bunch of us were sitting around playing cards and J decided he was going to move his wall locker. I asked him if he needed some help but he said 'Naw man I got it.' He thought he had it. J started moving that cabinet but he must have lost his grip or something because the next thing we heard was a big bang when the cabinet hit the floor. Everybody stopped and turned around to make sure he was alright. This bama was still holding on to the cabinet smiling up at us talking' 'bout, 'okay maybe I did need some help'."

When Stephen finished his story, Raquel was laughing and feeling better about her brother's situation. She didn't notice when the doctor appeared in the waiting room. Stephen pointed in his direction to let her know they needed to find out what was going on with Jalen.

"Who is here for Jalen Gibson?"

Before Raquel and Stephen could get to the doctor, LaShawn and Gale were both standing in front of the doctor.

"What's wrong with him?" asked LaShawn.

"Well…"

Before the doctor could start, Raquel interrupted.

"Excuse me. I don't know who either one of you are but I am Jalen's sister and that is his mother. You need to back up."

Raquel took the doctor by the arm and guided him in the direction where her mother and father were sitting. The doctor began again, this time addressing Jalen's family and Stephen. Gale stood near enough to hear the doctor's diagnosis.

"Jalen is lucky. He didn't have a heart attack. What he had was a bad case of acid reflux."

"So it wasn't a heart attack?" asked Jalen's mother.

"No, it was actually a bad case of heartburn. After talking to Jalen, I think what he has is chronic heartburn, which is called acid reflux."

"Acid reflux can make you feel like you're having a heart attack?" asked Raquel.

"A lot of things can make you feel like you're having a heart attack. Gas, heartburn, he just has to watch what he eats and it's a good idea not to eat late and then lay right down. I'm going to keep him overnight to make sure nothing else is going on. You can go in and see him."

While the doctor spoke with the family, LaShawn slipped into Jalen's room to talk to him. Everyone was so engrossed in the doctor's explanation of acid reflux that no one saw her go into his room. Jalen was asleep when she walked over to his bed and took his hand in hers. She got teary eyed, looking at the I.V. tube that was running from his arm.

"Baby, I'm sorry. I didn't mean for this to happen. I was just so mad at you. I didn't know what else to do. I wish I could take it back."

Jalen turned his head to look at her.

"Take what back?"

LaShawn was surprised. She thought Jalen was asleep. He had heard everything she'd said.

"I, I…"

"What did you do?" Jalen asked, raising his voice and snatching his hand from her.

Before LaShawn could explain herself, Stephen and Raquel were walking through the door.

"What the hell are you doing in here?" asked Raquel.

"Jalen are you alright?" Gale asked, sliding pass Stephen to get to Jalen's bedside.

"I'm okay."

"You have a lot of nerve being here. He probably wouldn't be here if it weren't for you." Gale said, yelling at LaShawn.

"What did you do LaShawn?" asked Jalen.

"She poisoned you."

"What?"

"She called me after we all met at her house and said that she was going to teach you a lesson by poisoning you. Supposedly it was something that would just give you real bad cramps and make you throw up, not put you in the hospital."

"Oh my, God. She tried to kill my baby," Cried Jalen's mother.

Raquel dropped her purse on the floor and started toward LaShawn.

"Bitch!"

Stephen grabbed Raquel to keep her from hitting LaShawn.

"LaShawn get out and don't come anywhere near me again."

"Jalen, I…"

"You better get the fuck out of here. You too, all y'all a bunch of crazy bitches. Get out!" screamed Raquel.

LaShawn rushed out with Raquel still grabbing for her. Stephen held on tight to keep the hospital room from becoming a women's wrestling match. Gale dropped her head and left quietly. Stephen finally let go of Raquel and she calmed down. Jalen's mother made her way to the side of his bed.

"Baby, are you alright?"

"I'm okay, Ma. Whatever LaShawn tried to do has nothing to do with why I'm in here. I talked to the doctor. I just can't eat and lay down on certain food."

"So the playa almost got played," said Jalen's father, in a condescending tone.

"I guess the apple don't fall far from the tree," Jalen responded, with an obvious attitude that he was even there.

"J, man, what did you do to those women?" asked Stephen.

"It's a long story but the bottom line is, I'm done with both of them."

They sat around talking to Jalen until visiting hours were over. When everyone was gone, Jalen thought about what LaShawn's attempt at poisoning him. Because he had used and hurt so many women, he almost had to pay for it with his life. This was the second time in his life that money and greed had led him on a path to death. LaShawn's women's summit had actually been in Jalen's best interest. He was tired of living a multiple life. He had too many people to try and keep happy. Even though they were paying to be with him, and paying for his time, it had all become too stressful to keep up. Jalen knew he had to change the way he looked at women if there was any hope of him having a real relationship in the future. He closed his eyes and enjoyed the peace and quiet of the hospital room. He didn't have to worry about LaShawn banging on his door or Nina cutting his tires. He welcomed sleep. He would be released from the hospital tomorrow but tonight he would get a good night's sleep.

Jalen waited for the orderly to come with a wheelchair so that he could leave. Stephen was waiting downstairs in his car to take him home. He fussed with the nurse trying to persuade her that he didn't need a wheelchair. She argued back that it was hospital policy and he couldn't get around it.

"Look, I won't tell if you don't. I can catch the elevator downstairs without someone pushing me out."

"You sure? You could use the orderly as a bodyguard," The nurse said, slyly.

"What? Oh, you got jokes."

"Apparently you have more than jokes, women fighting over you in the hospital?" The nurse looked at Jalen slyly.

He knew that look. He could have her if he wanted. She was a nice looking woman. He could tell she had a cute little shape underneath her hospital scrubs.

"Whatever, wasn't nobody in here fightin'."

He walked up close to her. Close enough that he could smell the scent of Downy in her clothes.

"You gon' let me outta here or what? Maybe you just tryin' to keep me around for yourself."

The nurse handed Jalen his release papers and a business card. He looked at the back of the business card where she had written her number.

"You can go. Call me, after you call her."

She turned the card over in his hand and then left the room. Jalen looked down at the card again. The name on the front of the card read Dr. Sheila Wright, Psychiatrist. Jalen laughed. What did she think was wrong with him that she would give him the number to a psychiatrist? Jalen stuck the number in his pocket and grabbed his jacket. He walked out of the hospital room thinking it had been a close call.

The Root of All Evil

…let us cleanse ourselves from everything that can **defile our body or spirit**. And let us work toward complete holiness because we fear God.

2 Corinthians 7:1

Jalen looked at his watch. It was only 3:45 and his appointment wasn't until 4:00. He turned the business card over in his hand several times, still apprehensive about talking to a psychiatrist, but he knew he needed help. Maybe she would be able to help him understand why it seemed like things always went bad for him. He had tried to turn his life around twice, and he had, but Jalen knew he still wasn't on course. First it was drugs and money and now it was women and money. The one thing that continued to be a problem for him was money. He recognized that that he didn't know how to let it go. He looked down at his watch again. It was 3:50.

"Shit, I'm just gonna have to be a few minutes early."

Jalen walked into the waiting area of Dr. Wright's office. The receptionist was a young, pretty woman who looked like she was about twenty-five or twenty-six. She was scheduling an appointment with a patient over the telephone and acknowledged Jalen's presence with a smile. He was impressed with her. She was dressed professional and if she was the same person that had scheduled his appointment, he had expected someone older.

"Good afternoon. Can I help you?" she asked, after hanging up the telephone.

"Yes, my name is Jalen Gibson. I have a four o'clock appointment."

The woman checked her computer screen then handed Jalen a clipboard, with several forms attached.

"Fill these forms out for me and the doctor will be with you shortly."

Jalen took the clipboard then found a seat. The waiting area was calming. The walls, chairs and carpet were all some shade of brown and jazz music played softly in the background. Jalen zipped through the forms with no problem. To his knowledge there was no history of mental disease in his family. He had a few relatives that acted crazy but they had never been diagnosed as just crazy. He walked back up to the receptionist's desk and handed her the clipboard.

"You can have a seat. She should be ready for you shortly."

The woman took the forms off of the clipboard and disappeared behind the closed door. When she returned, she called Jalen into the doctor's office. The doctor walked over to him and shook his hand.

"Hello Jalen, I'm Dr. Wright."

"Hi."

"Have a seat."

She directed him to a leather chair and she sat in the leather chair across from it. Jalen rubbed his hands over his jeans. Dr. Wright could tell he was nervous.

"So why are you here today?"

Jalen continued to rub at his jeans.

"Last week I thought I was having a heart attack but it turned out to be a bad case of acid reflux."

"Okay."

"Well one of the nurses gave me your card and suggested I give you a call."

"For acid reflux?"

"No. Two women that I had been dealing with, at the same time, were at the hospital. They almost got into a fight."

"Oh, they found out about each other at the hospital?"

"No. Actually one of them found out about all of the women I was dating and they all met up at her house."

"Keep talking."

"Well the woman that called the meeting decided she wanted to teach me a lesson so she tried to poison me. When she found out I was in the hospital, she thought it was because of the poison and then all of a sudden she was sorry."

"How did she find out about the other women?"

"She went through my cell phone and called all of the numbers."

"Were you surprised that the other women were receptive to her?"

"Some of them yeah. Others, no. Women like drama, especially LaShawn. She's the one that tried to poison me. She's broken my car windows, keyed my car, she comes to my apartment any time of the day or night and bangs on the door or the windows. She's crazy."

"Maybe she thought she had a reason to act up like that."

"I'm sure she did. I know her feelings were hurt when she found out about the other women but damn, poison?"

"How many women were you involved with?"

Jalen thought for a minute. He didn't want to leave anyone out.

"Eight."

"Are you sleeping with all eight or are some of them just friends?"

"*Were*. I was sleeping with all of them. The night of their big meeting, most of them ended it with me and anyone who didn't I did. I was tired anyway. It had started taking a lot out of me trying to please so many women, trying to keep everybody happy."

"Why were you trying to please, as you say, so many women?"

"They were giving me money, buying me vehicles, apartments, jewelry, stuff like that. In exchange I had to have sex with them and listen to their problems. It just got to be too much."

"Why are you here? What do you hope to gain from talking to me?"

"I was asking myself the same question. I'm not sure. I mean I don't really feel like there is anything wrong but I know using women for their money isn't right. I guess LaShawn trying to poison me kind of opened my eyes a little. Something has to change. I've tried before but the money is good. You can't believe what women are willing to do just to have a man."

"Let's forget the women for a minute. Tell me about you. Where did you grow up? Where did you go to school? Did you play sports? Things like that."

Jalen repositioned himself in the comfortable leather chair. He leaned to his left, resting on the arm of the chair.

"I grew up in DC. I hung out with a bunch of dudes that really didn't have anything going on. Stealing was our occupation. When I was fifteen, my moms moved us to Capital Heights."

"You said us. You have siblings?"

"I have an older sister. It's always been me and my mother and my sister."

"Where's your father?"

Jalen's expression changed. It was evident that his father wasn't a pleasant subject. He leaned back in the chair and began rubbing his legs again.

"I *could* say that nigga was dead. Shit he might as well be. He has never been there for me and my sister, or my mother but you can't tell them that. They still trip over that nigga like he's a real part of our family. He lives around the corner with his family. He chose them over us."

"Were your parents married?"

"Yeah they were married. For all I know they might still be married. I've never asked but when we were younger he just up and left. He told my mother he couldn't handle a family."

"Do you have any interaction with him?"

"When he decides to come around I speak. That's about it. Too much more and it usually ends in an argument. I don't know what it is but he has this thing that makes my mother and sister believe the bullshit he says. Even though he hurts them and disappoints them, time and time again, they still believe his bullshit."

The doctor looked down from time to time as Jalen talked, taking notes of their meeting.

"How is your relationship with your mother?"

"She's been very supportive of me even through my dumb shit. I accidentally overdosed in the tenth grade. A psychiatrist came to see me in the hospital and told me I needed to talk to somebody but I wasn't trying to hear it. I got myself together after that and started doing better in school but I had wasted so much time, it ended up taking me six years to finish high school instead of four."

"I guess the important thing is that you decided to finish. What did you do when you got out of school?"

"I went in the service. That was probably the best decision I have ever made in my life."

"Why is that?"

117

"It helped me to really get myself together. Like the commercial says, it helped me 'be all I can be'. I turned my life around and got my head clear of all the stealing and drug mess."

"So you were a good soldier?"

"I was one of the best. When I was in basic training, I received the Commanding General's Award and when I was stationed in Germany, I received the two Battalion medals of Excellence."

"Wow, that's quite an achievement. So when did you start getting involved with so many women?"

Jalen stretched his legs out and crossed them at the ankles, then crossed his hands over his stomach, getting more comfortable.

"When I was stationed in Kansas I met this woman. She was a fine ass redbone from Atlanta. We hung out one night, had a good time, then we ended up at her place. We had sex that night which was a Monday. By Friday she was asking me to move in with her. We were fuckin' like rabbits. This girl blew my mind. It was all about me when we had sex. I think I can honestly say she is the first person I ever made love to."

"You loved her?"

"No! I didn't say I loved her. I said she was the first person I ever made love to."

"I'm confused. How can you make love to someone you don't even love?"

"It was slow and passionate, caring."

"Okay, but I think you used a more appropriate word, passionate. Jalen, I don't believe you can physically make love to a person and not love them. When one or both of the people are passionate then definitely it makes for some great sex. So what happened to that relationship?"

"She was happy because I was attentive. I was happy because she bought me things. You name it and she didn't have a problem getting it for me. Eventually I got tired of it, her. I was ready to come back home. I finished up my four years and came back home."

"What does your relationship with that woman have to do with you sleeping with so many women?"

"I didn't do anything different or spectacular with her than I had done with women before but she acted like my penis was gold or something. The fact that she would give me whatever I wanted got me thinking that if she would do whatever other women probably would too, and they did."

"Did you ever feel bad? Like you were taking advantage of them?"

"I didn't do anything different from what women do all the time. When a woman meets a man, the first thing she thinks is 'what can I get out of him?' So why shouldn't I feel the same way? What can I get out of them? They wanted sex, I wanted money."

"At any point did you ever feel fulfilled?

"No, but at that time I wasn't looking for a woman to fulfill me, just pay my bills. That's what I got, women that would pay my bills and give me money."

"How were you able to keep consistency? I

121

mean keeping names and stories straight. And what about actually dating these women? Did you ever take them out or was it just sex?"

"It was just sex for me but I would take them out sometimes."

"Weren't you scared one of your other women would catch you out?"

"No. I knew what was going on with everybody. As far as keeping stories straight, it wasn't that hard. These were hard working women that didn't do a lot of partying or going out so I didn't really have that to worry about. I kept things tight. If I found out that one of them were cheating on me or even talking to another man they were cut. I didn't want to hear her crying or no explaining, it was just over."

Dr. Wright looked at the clock on the wall. Time had gone by quickly. She waited for Jalen to finish his thought before she ended their session.

"Jalen, I think you would definitely benefit from future sessions with me."

"Has it been an hour already?"

"Once you open up and really start talking, time does seem to fly by."

She closed her notebook and sat forward in her chair.

"I'd like you to think about some things. I think you have some issues with both of your parents that you need to deal with. The womanizing for money, I don't think we got to the root of that in this session but there is definitely a reason why you use women and then walk away feeling unfulfilled."

Jalen was quiet, thinking about the doctor's quick analysis of his life. She waited for him to respond. When he didn't she continued.

"What do you think? Do you think there is anything to be gained by seeing me again?"

"Yeah, I guess. I'm just processing what you said about the root of the problem."

He finally stood and extended his hand to the doctor.

"Yeah, I'll be back. What about next week?"

"I'm not sure what my schedule looks like. Talk to my assistant and she will get you on the calendar."

She shook his hand and smiled at him warmly. Jalen scheduled his next appointment then left. He rode home feeling anxious about his next meeting with the doctor. He had never talked that much to a woman or shared details of his life. He was usually the one listening. He had become accustomed to listening to his women but he had never felt comfortable opening up to them. He felt comfortable talking to the doctor. At first he thought maybe it would be a better idea to go and see a male psychiatrist but it was women that he continued to hurt so maybe it was a woman's insight that he needed.

On his next visit to the doctor's office, Jalen talked more in depth about his drug use and the overdose. The doctor suggested that he was hiding or running away from something. Jalen thought it was interesting, the psychiatrist in the hospital had told him the same thing. Jalen talked about his father and how much of a loser Jalen thought he was because he had left them. He also talked about how his mother was different with him than with his sister. After saying it, he dismissed it away, saying that it was probably because of all of the trouble he had been in as a teenager. At the end of the session, Dr. Wright suggested he talk to his mother, father, and sister and tell them how he felt. Jalen didn't disagree with the doctor but he wasn't ready for any long conversation with his father.

He took the first step and talked to his mother. Jalen sat down at the table with his mother and apologized for all of the trouble he had been when he was younger, and for not living up to her expectations. To his surprise, she hugged him and told him he had surpassed her expectations. She admitted that after his drug overdose she didn't expect him to make anything out of his life. She cried and then he cried. It was an emotional release for them both. He decided to have a few drinks with his sister. They laughed about when they were kids. After a few beers, Jalen felt like he had Raquel loosened up, and he had enough nerve to apologize for any wrong he had done to her in the past. Raquel talked trash to him and told him he had been a fuck up but she was glad he was now a responsible adult. Jalen sat back in his chair, his hand on his beer and his head down. He felt lighter, like the burden of his wrong doings had been lifted. His mother and his sister had always been the most important people in his life. Jalen felt like he could start all over with them.

Jalen sat in the leather chair across from Dr. Wright. She could tell he was excited about their session. He had just sat down and hadn't started talking yet but he was fidgety. She could tell he was ready to talk.

"Well, you look like you've had a good week. What's going on?"

"I did like you suggested. I talked to my mother and my sister."

"How did it go?"

"Better than I thought. I was afraid we'd end up in an argument but it was okay. My mother actually said she was proud of me."

Jalen smiled brightly as he talked about his mother.

"And my sister, we had a few beers, I apologized, she cussed me out...then called me a responsible adult. You were right. I do feel better. It helped apologizing for all my dumb decisions."

"What about your father? How did that go?"

Jalen was quiet. He looked away from her and out the window. He hadn't met with his father because he didn't feel like he was ready.

"I don't have anything to apologize to him for."

"Your conversation with him is going to be different than your conversation with your mother and sister. Maybe what you need is for him to apologize to you. Give him the opportunity. Who knows, maybe he wants to apologize but he just doesn't know how."

"Whatever, I'm not ready for that one."

Jalen's jaw was tight. He looked down at his pants and began to rub his legs like he always did when he was nervous or agitated. So she decided to change the subject.

"Jalen, how were you in school with girls? Were you the playa you are now?"

"No, not really. I could have been. I mean I played ball and hustled. Back then that's all it took to get a girl."

"Oh, you played football in school?"

"Naw, I played basketball in school for a while. I had scouts coming out looking at me and everything, but I couldn't keep my grades up so I got kicked off the basketball team."

"How did you feel about that?"

"I was mad at first but I was making so much money it really didn't matter."

"So you were a basketball jock and a big time hustler. Does that mean the girls were all over you?"

"I really wasn't into girls too much then. I was more on making money."

"That's interesting. Usually young guys with a lot of money use it to get the girls."

"I don't know. I always felt like girls were just users. They always want to be in charge. I dated a few girls in high school but as soon as they came with some shit like they were running something, I cut their ass back. They weren't putting any money in my pocket, why should I let them run me?"

"It sounds like you have some hidden animosity about women. Did something happen when you were a child? Were you ever molested?"

"What? No!"

"Jalen, it's alright. You would be surprised how many young boys have been assaulted and they don't even know it."

"I said I've never been molested."

"I believe your issues with women stem from something that has happened to you in the past. I could be wrong but that's what it sounds like to me."

Jalen didn't say anything. He looked out the window and rubbed his legs. After a few minutes of silence had passed, he dropped his head and began his story.

"I was twelve. I was walking home from school when these two girls walked up beside me. I don't know who they were, I had never seen them before. One of them

asked me if I was a virgin. I couldn't
believe it. I was only twelve, of course I
was a virgin. I guess they must have
thought I was older or something. I was big
for my age. One girl wrapped her arm
around one of my arms and the other one got
my other arm. They kept laughing. I was
trying to figure out what they were laughing
about. One girl rubbed my cheek and told
me we were gonna have fun. We were a
couple of blocks away from my house when
they pulled me into an alley. I wasn't scared
or anything, I was just confused. I didn't
know what they were planning to do. There
was an old mattress in the alley that
someone had thrown out. The girl that had
rubbed my face pushed me down on the
mattress and straddled me. She started
rubbing my penis. She rubbed her hand

over it a couple of times then squeezed it. My dick was hard as shit but I still wasn't sure what they were planning to do. The other girl didn't say anything she just kept looking around like she was keeping watch. The girl that was doing all the feeling pulled my dick out and started stroking it."

"What did you do?" The doctor interrupted.

"Nothing, I just let her do it. She pulled her skirt up and just sat down on me. She slid back and forth a couple of times and I came. She got up, pulled her skirt down then her and her girlfriend walked away laughing at me. I heard the girl say 'did you see how small his dick was?' They left me there with my dick out."

"How did you feel?"

"It was the most embarrassing thing that has ever happened to me. I was humiliated. Maybe that's why sex was never a big deal to me when I was a teenager. I ain't never really thought much of women since then."

"Why is that?"

"Because just like that girl used me eventually I came to realize that all women are users, and somehow sex is always attached. All of the women that I have ever dealt with have paid for me to have sex with them."

"So because they didn't mind giving you money you thought less of them?"

"They should have thought more of themselves."

"It sounds like a win-win situation to me. They gave you money and you gave them pleasure."

"It wasn't just money. Women have bought me cars, paid for apartments, clothes, jewelry, you name it, and they didn't all want me to do it to them. One chick would pay me to let her suck my dick. Honestly, I think they were all a bunch of lonely bitches."

"A bunch of lonely women that you took advantage of."

"Me? I didn't take advantage of anybody. They knew what they were doing."

"But were you up front with them about what you wanted?"

"Yes, I let them know what I would and wouldn't go for. For a while I only dealt with married women because I didn't want to be attached. Then when they started acting crazy, banging on my door in the middle of the night, cutting tires and breaking windows, I had to change it up. But I always let them know where I was coming from. It was my way or the highway, and if I thought for a minute that you had slept with someone else, you were cut off."

Jalen laughed at himself.

"I guess that's kind of messed up, right? I would even carry the married women like that too. Sometimes I would get them to sneak out of bed with their husbands and come around the corner and do it to me in my car."

He laughed again, a sly laugh, then looked out the window. His look was solemn.

"What are you thinking?" The doctor asked.

"I've screwed up a lot of women's lives."

She gave him a minute to finish his thought.

"Jalen, I think we've finally found the root of the problem. When those girls pulled you into that alley and raped you, they stole so many things from you. Your innocence, your first kiss, your right to choose who you wanted to be your first. Plainly put they took away your power. Rape isn't about sex. It's about power."

"I understand what you're saying but I heard the girl when they were walking away. She figured I was a little boy with a little dick compared to her boyfriend."

"It was still about power. She picked you for a reason. You were younger than her so she felt she could dominate you. You could have hit her."

"My mother taught me never to hit women."

"That's my point. That girl took advantage of you when you were twelve and you've been getting back at women ever since. You said your mother used to talk about your father like he was all that even though he left. That just added to your negative outlook on women. You apologized to your mother, that was a good start, but now you have to atone for all the hurt you caused those women."

"How do you suggest I do that? Call them?" he asked, sarcastically.

"That would be a good start."

"Are you kidding me? I can't even remember the names of all the women I've slept with."

"Well then just concentrate on the present. You don't have to go way back in the past. How about the women who attended the 'waiting to exhale' party, as you put it? Apologize to them, and then let go of the past. Then you can start new."

"I don't know if I can do that."

"Just think about it. Our time is up but we made a lot of progress today. How do you feel?"

"I don't know, just trying to take it all in."

Jalen stood up and walked to the door. He stopped with his hand on the doorknob.

"I have a lot to apologize for."

Dr. Wright walked over and put her hand on his shoulder.

"Just take your time."

Jalen rode home thinking hard about his session with Dr. Wright. He formulated a list of names in his mind. Then he began to separate them. One list consisted of women he had decided to call to apologize. Everybody else would get an e-mail or letter in the mail. Jalen smiled, pleased with himself. When the doctor first suggested he call the women, Jalen couldn't imagine going through with something like that. Now it seemed doable. Ultimately, a small price to pay to live a more peaceful, drama-free life.

When Jalen got home, he got a piece of paper and wrote down the names in separate columns the way he had decided to do in the car. Jalen dialed the numbers that he knew by heart. He dialed the first number and got an answering machine. Relieved that he didn't have to talk to the woman, he left a quick message telling her that he was sorry for any heartache he had caused her, then hung up.

"This might be easier than I thought," Jalen said, dialing the next number.

The next call wasn't as easy.

"Hello."

"Sabrina this is Jalen. You got a minute?"

She didn't respond. There was silence for a few seconds that he took to mean she was giving him a chance to say whatever he needed to say.

"I called to apologize. I know I hurt you and…"

Before Jalen could say another word, Sabrina interrupted him.

"Jalen, I don't know why you are doing this but you can keep your apology. I loved you and there wasn't anything I wouldn't have done for you but you weren't ready for that. You weren't ready for a woman like me. Yes, I was hurt when you broke it off, but I've gotten past that. I don't accept your apology and don't call me anymore."

Jalen heard a click and then a dial tone. She had hung up before he could say anything else. Jalen knew talking to some of them wouldn't be easy but he thought he was starting with the women who he had caused the least hurt. Now he wasn't sure he would be able to finish the calls. Part of him was sorry, and part of him just didn't want to hear the whining or crying that was sure to come. He finally decided to just send everybody on the list a letter. Jalen wrote what he thought was a heartfelt sincere apology.

As I look back, I can't help but to think about all of the good times that we shared. I know that if I had been able to appreciate you, we would have experienced more of those good times. I'd like to take this opportunity to say thank you. You have shown me so much patience and understanding. Even when I acted like I didn't care, and my unwillingness to let go and allow things to happen, you stayed consistent in showing me how someone who claims to love you should act. I apologize for all of the moments of emptiness that I am

sure I caused you. I have been struggling,
trying hard to figure out what I am longing
for in a relationship, but what I've been
experiencing spiritually, emotionally is that
every time I try, I only seem to make matters
worse. In an effort to live a better life, I am
trying to clean up the messes I have made in
the past. Please forgive me. I hope now we
can both go on with our lives and have
closure.

 Sincerely,

 Jalen

Jalen printed a copy of the letter for each of the women on his list. After he sealed the last envelope, he sat back in his chair and exhaled deeply. He felt like a burden had been lifted off his shoulders. Jalen felt like his life was taking a turn for the better, one more time. He bowed his head and thanked God for delivering him from himself one more time.

Atonement

In whom we have redemption through
His blood, the **forgiveness** of sins, according
to the riches of His grace.

Ephesians 1:7

A week had passed and Jalen had only gotten one phone call about his letter, for that he was glad. He almost didn't answer the telephone when he saw LaShawn's number. Somehow he knew she would be the one to respond. She had been harder to shake than anyone else. Jalen remembered when they first started hanging out.

Jalen had watched her walk to his side of the bar. He saw her big hips and legs as soon as she walked in. She was wearing a pair of jeans and a tight fitting t-shirt. He locked eyes with her for a moment and then looked away. He knew that was all it took to get her to sit next to him. He was right. She rested her purse on the hook under the bar between her legs and sat down on the stool next to Jalen.

He was sitting at the bar at Jasper's in Greenbelt, watching the Wizards lose to the Pistons, and sipping a beer.

"Hi, how you doin'?"

Jalen looked over at her and smiled.

"Hi."

"Can I have a Heineken?"

Jalen smiled, he thought it was cute, an attractive woman sitting at the bar drinking a beer.

"Can I buy the next one?" Jalen asked.

"Sure, thank you."

"No problem. I think it's kind of cute, a woman at the bar drinking a beer."

"Why? Are beers reserved for men?" she asked, smiling.

"No, but women usually order martini's, or margarita's, something cute."

"I don't like sweet drinks."

"You prefer a tall cold one, huh?"

"No, I prefer a tall hot one," she said, taking a sip of her beer and smiling slyly.

At that point, Jalen knew what direction she was trying to take the conversation. Before he left, he knew he would have her number and before long have her in his bed.

"I'm Jalen. What's your name?"

"LaShawn."

"Why are you by yourself? Where's your man?"

"He's at work."

"Oh you do have a man?"

"I'm married," she said, flashing her ring at Jalen.

Jalen had seen the ring before she flashed it at him. It made her more interesting to him. Jalen looked at married women as challenges. They always proclaimed how happy they were at home, and my husband this and that, until they were laid up in his bed, calling his name instead of their man's.

"Are you happy?"

"Most of the time."

Jalen was surprised by her response. She was going to be easier than he thought.

"Most of the time? What would it take to make you happy all of the time?"

"He works too much so sometimes I feel like I need some attention."

"What kind of attention do you need?"

LaShawn smiled that sly smile again and took a sip of her beer.

"What about you? Are you married?"

Jalen let the question slide. He knew he already had her. There was no need for him to press her.

"No I'm not married. I haven't found the right woman."

Jalen always threw that comment out as a hook. It was his standard pickup line. He knew women loved a challenge and the thought that they could do something some other woman couldn't. He swallowed the last of his beer then put a twenty dollar bill on the bar. The bartender picked up the twenty and held it up, waiting for Jalen to signal whether or not he needed change. Jalen gave him a hand wave letting him know to keep the change.

"Give her one more. Keep the rest."

"Leaving so soon? I just got here."

"I gotta role. It was nice talking to you."

Jalen walked away before she could say anything else. When she reached for her beer she noticed that he had left his number. LaShawn smiled and put the number in her purse, knowing she would call soon.

LaShawn was curious about Jalen but she tried not to call. However, her willpower didn't last too long. She called a week later. They met for drinks then ended up in bed at his apartment. Jalen listened to LaShawn talk about how her husband neglected her and that their sex life was nearly non-existent. Then he fucked her brains out. Jalen couldn't believe his eyes when he saw the tears flowing from LaShawn's eyes when she came. Once again, he felt like he was the man. She pulled Jalen to her and held him there. He had no idea what he had gotten himself into.

After sleeping with Jalen for four months, LaShawn told Jalen she was in love

with him and planning to leave her husband.
Jalen immediately tried to talk her out of it.
He said everything he could think of but she
was insistent. Jalen finally broke it off with
her and told her to never call him again.
Jalen knew she wouldn't take the break up
well but he had no idea how much it would
cost him. She broke the windows in his car,
cut his tires, banged on his apartment door
in the middle of the night screaming curse
words at him. He finally filed a restraining
order against her. She showed up to court
wearing a plain grey skirt, a white buttoned
down blouse, and her hair pinned up. She
told the judge that she had been drawn into
an adulterous relationship with Jalen and
after he was done using her to pay his bills,
he was adding insult to injury by filing a
false complaint against her. She sounded so

sincere that if Jalen hadn't known better, he would have believed her. The judge dismissed Jalen's case and warned him against filing any further false complaints. LaShawn showed up at Jalen's apartment after court and begged her way in. She pleaded with him to forgive her and take her back. After promising to stay with her husband, he took her back and things went back to the way they had been before, her paying and him taking.

Jalen answered the telephone reluctantly.

"Hello."

"Hi. I got your letter."

LaShawn paused and Jalen waited.

"I accept your apology. I wish we could start over."

"LaShawn, like I said in the letter I'm trying to change my life. That means doing different."

"I know. I was just saying, I wish things could have been different. If I wasn't married when we met…"

Jalen stopped her.

"But you were and I was wrong for ever getting involved with you. I'm sorry I took advantage of you."

"I'm not sorry. I'm not sorry for anything I ever gave you or did for you. I did them out of love. I will always love you."

"LaShawn, if you love me you will let this go. We have to move on. You need to concentrate on your husband, not me. Thank you for accepting my apology. You don't know how much that helps me, but if

156

you really love me, you'll just let me go. I
wish you nothing but happiness. Good-
bye."

Jalen hung up the telephone and
exhaled. He prayed she wouldn't call back.
She didn't.

Dr. Wright could tell it had been a busy
week for Jalen. He sat down and
immediately started rubbing his legs and
acting antsy.

"Jalen, what's going on? Is everything
okay? You look very anxious today."

"It's been a helluva week."

"Why, what happened?"

"I did like you suggested and
apologized to some of the women in my
past."

"How'd it go?"

"Well, at first I was going to call some of them but after I got laid out, I decided to write a letter and send that. I think all of them should have gotten it but I only got one call."

"Go ahead."

"It was LaShawn. The same girl that tried to poison me."

"What did she say?"

"It sounded like she wanted us to hook back up."

"How did you feel about that?"

"She's married. I'm coming to see you to try and change my life. It would be a waste if I go back to my old ways. I told her she needs to work on her marriage."

"Good for you. How did she respond?"

"I said what I had to say and hung up. Luckily she didn't call back, but you know what?"

"What?"

"You were right, again. I did feel better after I wrote that letter, and I felt even better when I put them in the mail. I was glad nobody called me. I started not to answer LaShawn's call but I figured I owed her at least that much. I feel bad for her. I hope she can get it together."

"Well, it sounds like you had a very productive week. I'm sure you will start to see a change as you release these old issues."

"Like I said, I'm starting to feel lighter."

"I have to ask, have you talked to your father?"

"Doc, give me a break. I can't do but so much at one time."

"You're right. I'm just asking."

They laughed and continued the conversation. Jalen talked about work, his mother, and hanging out with some friends. Dr. Wright could tell that their sessions were helping him. She felt like she had made enough progress with Jalen that she no longer needed to see him every week. When the session was over, she let him know that she would be off for a while and that her assistant would call to schedule an appointment with him when she returned. Jalen had started to look forward to his meetings with her. He was disappointed, knowing he wouldn't see her for a few weeks. She had been the only woman he had talked to for the past month and a half

and he agreed with her when she said he had
made a lot of progress, but he knew he
would miss talking to her. Jalen left the
doctor's office feeling like he had something
else to say but he decided to keep it to
himself for now.

Jalen's time was split between work and
home. He had no desire to go out and pick
up women. The women on his job that were
used to his flirtatious remarks were surprised
when Jalen didn't have anything to say
except good morning. He just didn't feel
like it. He felt no desire for sex including
conversation. Instead, he waited patiently
for Dr. Wright to return. When her assistant
finally called to schedule his appointment,
he was so excited he could hardly wait to
meet with her. His appointment was for

Friday but the rest of the week dragged. It seemed like Friday would never come.

Jalen sat down in what had become *his* chair. He wasn't rubbing his legs or looking over anxious like he usually did at the beginning of their sessions. Dr. Wright noticed how calm he looked. It was just more confirmation for her that Jalen was making progress.

"So, how have you been?" she asked.

"I'm good."

"You look good. You look calm. What have you been up to since our last meeting?"

"Nothing, just working. Waiting for my therapist to get back from vacation. You are the only person I really have to talk to."

"You have friends."

"Yeah but I have never been able to open up to anyone the way that I've opened up to you. I don't know what it is."

"I have listened to you without judging you. That has allowed you the freedom to open up."

"No, I think it's more than that. I've been thinking about seeing you ever since our last session."

Dr. Wright could hear where the conversation was going and she wasn't going to allow it. It was normal for patients to feel like there was some kind of relationship developing. In all actuality, there was a relationship developing, just not the type of relationship the patient envisioned.

"Have any other women called?"

Jalen paused. He understood that she was trying to keep things professional. He went with it.

"No, no one else has called. I'm glad. I think it means everyone has moved on."

"Well that's good. What about your family?"

"I have talked to my mother a couple of times and my sister and I have always been okay so we're cool."

"What about your father?"

Jalen's face changed. His father was always a touchy subject.

"I haven't talked to him."

"I was hoping to come back and hear all about that conversation."

"I'm not ready for that."

"Sure you are. You didn't think you were ready to talk to your mom and sister, or write those letters, but you did. You said it yourself that you felt better after you did. I promise you, you will experience an ever greater relief after that conversation."

Jalen understood what she was saying but he still didn't think he was ready. Dr. Wright continued to talk to Jalen trying to make him understand that he would have to talk to his father in order to be free. He resisted through the entire session until their time was finally up.

"I hope you really consider what I'm telling you."

Jalen and the doctor stood up to say their good-byes. Jalen walked over to the door to leave and the doctor followed. Before he opened the door, he turned around to finish the conversation he had started earlier.

"I can't stop thinking about you. Do you think we can get together outside of our sessions?"

"Jalen…"

"I know you think it's because you're my doctor and you're helping me get my shit together but it's more than that."

"Jalen, if I wasn't your therapist maybe things would be different but it is what it is. I have to ask you to respect that."

Jalen searched her face for some sign that she really wanted him and that she was using professionalism as an excuse, but he didn't see it. Instead he leaned over and kissed her on her cheek. She allowed it.

"I got you. I guess I'm growing up. I'll see you next week."

Jalen left feeling a sense of satisfaction. The doctor had shot him down but he didn't feel rejected. He understood about the whole doctor patient thing. After some thought he even understood what the doctor was saying about him being attracted to her because she listened and responded unconditionally. When he first started seeing her, he had no idea their sessions would help him get to a place of peace. She had been right in everything she had told him. Jalen knew he needed to have a conversation with his father and get some things off his chest. Up to now, he felt like he wasn't ready for it. He knew he couldn't put it off forever and if it would be one more thing to help get rid of his past hurts and regrets, he would man up, and just do it. Tomorrow was as good a day as any.

Jalen called his father and asked if they could meet. He was honest when his father

asked him what he wanted to meet about.
Jalen told his father that he had some issues
he wanted to get off his chest so that maybe
one day they would be able to develop
something that resembled a father-son
relationship. Jalen's father was reluctant at
first. Whenever he and Jalen were in the
same room, they usually ended up arguing,
but Clyde could hear a difference in his
son's tone and voice so he agreed. He told
Jalen to meet him at his job and he would
talk to him on a break. Clyde felt like work
would be a safe zone. If the conversation
started to get out of hand or go in a direction
that he didn't like he could just get up and
go back to work. Jalen agreed to meet his
father at his job. He would have preferred a
place with more privacy but he wasn't going
to argue the point. He wanted to get it over

with before he changed his mind about it being a good idea. When he pulled into the parking lot he called his father to let him know he was there. Jalen had to leave his driver's license at the front desk and sign in. When Jalen saw his father he tried to look at him differently. He had always been the enemy in Jalen's mind. This time he greeted his father with a hand shake and a hug. Clyde was stunned. It had been years since the last time his son had embraced him.

"I'm on a break so we can go in the break room and talk."

Clyde led Jalen down the hall and into an empty break room. Jalen was pleasantly surprised that no one else was hanging out in the break room. He wasn't comfortable with the thought of pouring his heart out in front of strangers. It was going to be hard enough for him to open up to his father, not knowing what his reaction would be. Clyde pointed to a table then motioned for Jalen to sit down.

"You want some coffee, a soda, or something?"

"Naw I'm good," said Jalen.

"I'ma get me some coffee. What you wanna talk about? My break is only fifteen minutes."

Jalen was a little irritated that he only had fifteen minutes to set things straight with a man that he usually didn't want to have anything to do with.

"I've been seeing a therapist," Jalen started.

"Why, what's wrong with you?" Clyde interrupted.

"I got tired of the way my life was going. All the women, especially that last episode in the hospital. I decided to go and talk to someone. Find out why I can't keep a good woman and maintain a relationship."

"What does any of this have to do with me?"

"My therapist suggested I try and repair my past relationships including talking to Momma and Raquel, and you. I have been mad at you for most of my life. It's been more of a burden than I realized. I want, no I need to forgive you for not being in my life the way I thought you should have been. I need to forgive you for not being a good father."

"So you came here to tell me I ain't shit to you?"

"No, that's not why I'm here. Like I said I'm trying to get my self together and let go of old shit. We've never been close and I'm not looking to start over but I would like to at least be friends."

"Friends? What you want to hang out, drink beers, talk shit?" he asked, mocking Jalen.

Jalen readjusted himself in his chair. He was beginning to get irritated. While Jalen made an attempt at bonding, his father decided to be a smartass.

"Naw, man. We don't have to hang out. If you don't mind, I'll just call you from time to time. If you're available, maybe we can get a beer *from time to time*."

Clyde looked at Jalen. He had become accustomed to arguing with Jalen. He had reserved himself to the thought that he would never be friends with his son, but here he was seemingly trying to change that.

"Alright."

"So we cool?"

"Yeah, we good."

Jalen stood up and extended his hand to his father. Clyde stood up and shook his hand. Jalen pulled him into him and hugged him. He hugged him back.

"Clyde, what's going on? Who is this?" Shirley was one of his father's co-workers. She was a short stout woman with a wide smile. Jalen looked at her and smiled.

"Oh, this is my son."

Jalen felt a sense of pride. It was the first time he had ever heard his father acknowledge him.

"Your son? I thought you were away in school. Did you graduate?"

Jalen was confused. He hadn't gone to college. He had graduated from high school and gone into the army. She apparently had him confused with someone else.

"No, ma'am, I'm not in school."

"Clyde you told me your son was in college."

It dawned on Jalen that the woman must have been talking about his father's girlfriend, Pam's son, Mark. Mark was twenty years old and had attended a semester at Hampton, until he got caught selling weed on campus. He was expelled and had to do eight months in a State of Virginia prison. Obviously, his father talked about Mark as if he was his only son.

"No, ma'am. I wasn't away in school. I'm his son, Jalen."

"Oh?"

The woman's surprise was obvious.

"Yeah, this is my oldest son."

"Oh, I'm sorry I didn't know you had more than one son. Hi Jalen it's nice to meet you."

Shirley shook Jalen's hand then walked over to the microwave to pop a bag of popcorn.

"Look, I gotta get back to work."

"Okay, I was leaving anyway. Thanks for talking to me."

Jalen was ready to leave. He had done what he had come to do. His father hadn't given him the best reception but something was better than nothing. Jalen signed out of the log-in book at the front door and retrieved his license. He didn't even bother to look behind him to see if his father was still there. He got in his car and drove home. A part of him felt a small relief for having told his father how he felt, but the other part of him wanted to call him back on the telephone and cuss him out. It all started with the phone call to his father. Why would he suggest having a meaningful conversation on his job while he was on his fifteen-minute break? Then Shirley suggesting that he was Mark because his father talked about Mark as if he was the only son he had, and to add insult to injury Mark wasn't even his son. Jalen felt himself getting worked up. He took a deep breath, then exhaled. As much as he wanted things to change some things never would. As easy as it was to stay mad at his father, Jalen decided to let it go. He had said he would call his father from time to time but now it didn't matter if he talked to him at all. The bottom line was that he did feel better with or without his father's help. Jalen's mind went back to Dr. Wright. He couldn't wait for his next appointment. He felt like he needed to unload and she was the only person he could talk to.

Jalen locked his car and dropped his keys in his pocket and looked at his watch. He was a few minutes early as usual for his appointment with Dr. Wright.

"Excuse me? Is your name Jalen Gibson?"

Jalen looked puzzled. He didn't recognize the man as someone he knew.

"Yeah, do I know you?"

"I'm LaShawn's husband. I know you've been sleeping with my wife. She left me because she says she's in love with you and that she just can't get you out of her system. Do you realize we have kids?"

Jalen was stunned. He couldn't believe
LaShawn had told her husband about them.
Jalen remembered his last conversation with
her. He had no idea she would leave her
husband. The letter was meant to end it all.

"Hey, man, I'm sorry. Really. I was
wrong for getting involved with LaShawn
but I ended it. She mentioned something
about leaving but I told her she needed to
stay home with her family. I had no
intention of breaking up your family."

"No intention? Don't act like you give
a damn about my family."

The man had tears running down his
cheeks.

"I love my wife. There isn't anything I wouldn't do to keep her. I am determined to keep my family together."

"I'm not trying to break up your family."

Before Jalen could say another word, the man had pulled a gun. He didn't say another word. He pulled the trigger three times shooting Jalen at close range. When Jalen's body hit the ground, the man dropped his hand to his side and walked away. Jalen felt his body going numb. He blinked his eyes praying to God to keep him alive. Jalen wasn't sure how much time had passed before he heard the siren of the ambulance. A passerby noticed him laying on the ground and went over to help him. Jalen laid in the ambulance listening to the paramedic working to keep him alive. He looked over at the I.V. in his arm and the blood stained gauze in the paramedics hand. Jalen wiggled his fingers trying to get some feeling, but his fingers didn't move. The sound of the ambulance siren faded away.

"Hurry, his pulse is dropping."

The doctors worked frantically to stabilize Jalen. They couldn't operate and remove the bullets until he was stable.

"He's going into cardiac arrest."

"Check the monitor," yelled another doctor.

"Hand me the paddles."

One of the doctors started to pump Jalen's chest trying to stimulate his heart to get it pumping again while the other squeezed the air bag over his face in between pumps. One of the nurses in the room cut on the electric paddles and handed them to the doctor.

"Stand back," said the doctor.

He shocked Jalen's body but it didn't change the line on the monitor. Again, he shocked him, and again nothing.

"Turn it up."

The nurse turned up the power on the electric paddles. The doctor shocked Jalen again and again but still there was no pulse.

"That's it. We lost him."

The doctor handed the paddles to the nurse. The other doctor moved the stethoscope around on Jalen's chest, unwilling to accept defeat.

"Wait a minute. I think I got something."

The doctors worked together for what sounded like a faint pulse.

"Beep"

Everyone in the room breathed a sigh of relief when the monitor began again signaling Jalen's heartbeat.

"Whew! This guy is a fighter. Get him to surgery."

Jalen opened his eyes. He was surprised to see Dr. Wright sitting in the chair beside his bed. She was sitting patiently waiting for him to open his eyes.

"What are you doing here?"

"I told your mother I would watch you while she and your sister went to get something to eat."

Jalen tried to swallow but his mouth and throat were so dry he began to cough. Dr. Wright poured some water in the plastic cup on the table next to Jalen's bed.

"Your throat is probably sore from the tube they had down your throat during surgery. You are blessed to be alive. Do you know that?"

"I remember LaShawn's husband shooting me, and then the ride in the ambulance. I think I must have blacked out because when I woke up, I saw all these people around me but I couldn't talk. Then everything went black."

"They thought you were dead. The doctor said he shocked you over and over again but still didn't get a pulse. He was about to declare you dead when you came back."

Jalen put his hand on his chest. He was sure there must be a big bruise on his chest. It hurt too much for there not to be.

"Yeah, I guess I am blessed. The man upstairs just keeps looking out for me. They say he watches out for babies and fools."

"The police arrested LaShawn's husband."

"How did they catch him?"

"The woman that called the ambulance also called the police and gave them the tag number of his car."

"You know, I never felt bad when I was sleeping with married women. I didn't care about the man they had at home, but when LaShawn said she was leaving home for me I knew that wasn't something I wanted on my head. I tried to tell him that but he didn't believe me. Hell, I guess I wouldn't have believed me either."

"The police said that he confessed. He said he's been following you for weeks waiting for the right time to approach you."

"He waited patiently. I should be dead, but you know what...I feel bad for him. I looked in his eyes when he told me how much he loves LaShawn. He was so hurt. I caused that."

"It was a bad situation that could have been handled differently. You apologized to LaShawn..."

"Yeah, but the one I should have been apologizing to was her husband."

Jalen looked away from her feeling disgusted with himself. He felt ashamed. He had never loved a woman that way. Jalen's mother and sister walked into the room and rushed over to him when they saw that he was awake. Dr. Wright excused herself and left Jalen with his family. She was concerned that all the progress they had madder would go down the drain while he was in the hospital sulking over LaShawn's marriage, but she knew Jalen had to continue to face the demons of his past in order to move on to any kind of meaningful relationship.

Jalen limped into the courtroom leaning on his cane. He walked up to the podium to address the judge.

"Your Honor, I would like to ask the court to show Mr. Carver leniency."

"Mr. Gibson, wasn't it Mr. Carver that shot you?"

"Yes sir."

"Well why would you be here today at his sentencing asking for leniency for him?"

"It's my fault that he is even here today. I had an affair with his wife not for a moment considering the damage I was doing to their family. I was selfish for continuing the relationship even after she told me she wanted to leave her husband for me."

"That still doesn't change the law. Married people get into adulterous relationships every day. Men and women leave their husbands for a lover every day. Shooting your wife's lover is never the right solution."

"I know that sir but my reason for being here is more for me than him."

"What do you mean?

"I have a lot to apologize for. A lot to atone for and destroying this man's marriage is one. I hoped that by coming here and trying to convince you to go easy on him that somehow it would redeem me. Ultimately it is your decision on what happens to this man. I just hope that you take my words into consideration. Thank you."

Jalen walked away from the podium and took a seat in the back of the courtroom. He walked pass LaShawn, without looking at her. She was sitting behind her husband.

"Alvin Carver, please rise," The judge commanded.

Alvin stood up behind the defendant's table, waiting for the judge to sentence him. He couldn't believe Jalen had stood up on his behalf. He was a good man that loved his family. He was glad that Jalen hadn't died but at the time, he didn't see any other option.

"You were found guilty on the charge of aggravated assault. I have taken into consideration the things that Mr. Gibson said and so I'm not going to assign the maximum sentence. Instead I am going to give you an opportunity to help yourself and your family. I am ordering you to take anger management classes at a facility approved by this court. I am also ordering that you attend family counseling with your children and your wife. Although you said you love your family, you need to understand that every action you take has an affect on your children. Consider them the next time you think about doing something that will separate you from them. I can't force your wife to attend marriage counseling, but it would be a good idea if you plan to work on your marriage. I am placing you on probation for six months. If you do not comply in any way with this order, you will be arrested and put in jail for a term to be determined."

The judge racked his gavel and called for a recess. Jalen left the courtroom satisfied with the outcome. He had spoken with the prosecutor before the trial began and asked him to charge Alvin as light as possible, and now the judge also had listened and taken what he had said into consideration. Jalen slid down in the seat of his car and hooked his seatbelt. He finally felt a sense of relief. Dr. Wright had told him she would meet with him after he left court regardless of the time. Jalen started the car and put it in drive, and then he put it back in park and turned the car off. He closed his eyes and bowed his head. A

sharp pain shot through his leg. Jalen said a
quick prayer while he waited for the pain to
subside. Ever since he had been released
from the hospital, whenever the pain from
his gunshot wounds bothered him he took a
moment and thanked God that it was pain
and not death. Jalen lifted his head but
didn't start the car. He looked out the
window and inhaled, glad to be alive. He
thought over the bad things that had
happened to him in his life. Each time he
had been hurt, it was his own doing. Jalen
felt a lump in his throat. It was obvious that
God had a plan for his life. He was almost
afraid of what it could be. For God to save
him repeatedly there had to be something
bigger and better waiting for him. He turned
the key in the ignition and started the car.
He had no idea what the bigger and better

was but he knew that with God in his corner, anything was possible. Jalen knew he still had a lot of work to do on himself but he had crossed the most important hurdle of all. He finally realized that he was the problem. With Dr. Wright's help, and his faith in God, he was working on fixing the problem from the inside out. One day he would be a good, loving man to the right woman, but today, it was all about him.